THE HIGHWAY

Nebo's Journey Back to the Promised Land

Luisette Kraal

DEDICATION

This book is dedicated to the Moody Bible Institute. Thank you to my professors, Dr. J. Coakley and Dr. J. Wong Loi Sing, for teaching me the science of hermeneutics, the art of research and joy of the Old Testament.

A huge thanks to my dear husband Ed, my daughter Jo-Hanna, and my lovely boys, Symar, Timmy and Bryan.

CONTENTS

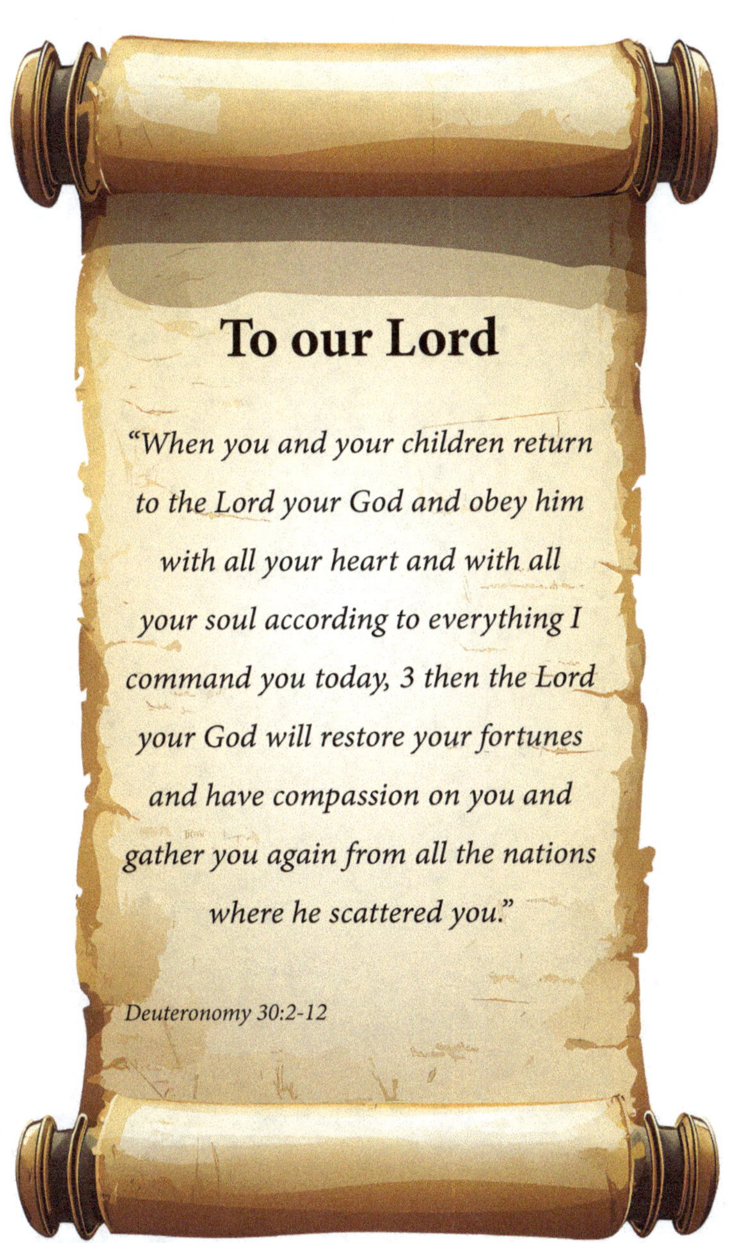

To our Lord

"When you and your children return to the Lord your God and obey him with all your heart and with all your soul according to everything I command you today, 3 then the Lord your God will restore your fortunes and have compassion on you and gather you again from all the nations where he scattered you."

Deuteronomy 30:2-12

CHAPTER 1

Nebo and Zaccai

ebo, a Jewish boy with black curly hair and a small olive brown face, stood on the rock and waved his arms in the air. "I'm invisible!" he hollered and jumped from the rock right in front of his friend Zaccai. Zaccai was a little younger than Nebo. He was a robust boy with short arms and legs. His shining brown round face was sweaty but he didn't pay attention to it. He was chasing his friend Nebo around the rock. He bellowed "I'm going to get you! I am a Philistines, and I'm a good fighter!" But Nebo was not letting his friend get away with it so quickly and he shouted back "I am a Jew. I have God on my side. I'm going to win." And he did outrun Zaccai.

Panting and sweating, they later sat on the kitchen floor to drink their sweet cow milk. It was a good day. A fun day. "That was fun," said Zaccai panting, while he wiped the sweat from his face and drank his milk.

Ima, Nebo's mother, ruffled his hair. "So Nebo made you work for it today," she teased Zaccai and he laughed.

"I will get him the next time," Zaccai said selfassuredly.

Ima laughed too. "Don't you need to help your father with the chores?" asked Ima.

"Well, I don't really need to help, I did my chores before playtime, but I guess I should go because it is almost time for supper. " He jumped up and said goodbye to his friend Zaccai.

"Bye Nebo, see you tomorrow and we will play soldiers again."

"I am sorry Zaccai, but Nebo cannot play tomorrow. He is starting classes in Hebrew and in the Torah, the Jewish Bible. He is a big boy now. He needs to know what our God wants us to do. Nebo's father already talked with your father. Maybe you can come too. We are going to the preacher Azariah to learn," said Ima.

"I will ask my father then!" Zaccai roared, as he ran toward his house that was on the same street.

Every day Nebo and Zaccai, the eight-year-old boys, played together. It was their favorite thing to do. They had many games they liked to play: hiding, throwing stones, playing board games, jumping, and of course, playing soldiers. That was the most fun of all. Nebo was turning nine now and Ah-bee, his father, wanted him to learn from the Torah. In the Torah, all the laws and commandments of Moses were written and all the people had to know them to be able to serve God. Nebo's father was a priest. People loved him and came from far to talk to him. But for Nebo he was just his Abba, his father. And Nebo lovingly called him Ah-bee. Ah-bee was a priest for all the Jews living in Babylon.

Ima called after Zaccai. "Say 'hi' to your mother. Tell her I will come by tomorrow."

Nebo was excited to go to the Hebrew Teacher. Nebo's father had many talks with the teacher Azariah and Nebo knew him well. "Ima," he said to his mother, "if I go to classes with teacher Azariah, Ah-bee might let me take part in the mantalks. Oh how exciting!" Nebo jumped up and down.

"I really hope Zaccai can go with me," he repeated over and over while he tried to get another cup of sweet milk from his mother.

The next day Nebo got bad news. Zaccai was not going to join the classes. Zaccai's father wanted Zaccai to learn to read and write Aramaic, numbers and business. Aramaic was the language people spoke in Babylon and Zaccai had to know Aramaic if he was going to take over his father's business one day.

The two boys sat with their backs leaning against the rock and talked about the future. "My father works in the palace of the King," said Zaccai, beaming with pride. "He wants me to learn about buying and selling and I need to know Aramaic for that. I cannot spent my time learning Hebrew for fun."

"It is not for fun!" said Nebo. "We are Jews, we need to know the language of our fathers, and we need to read our Bible, the Torah, in the original language. I am going to be a priest, just like my father so I need to know all of the law."

"Yehhh, I know, I know," said Zaccai. "You believe that we are still Jews but I am not sure. I was born in this country. My father was born here, and his father, Grandpa Olli, was born here so I think I am Babylonian. I am not a Jew anymore."

"Don't say that!" said Nebo with panic in his voice. He looked around to see if anyone had heard Zaccai's words. "Don't you ever say that, Zaccai. We are Jews. Our families are living in this country because, long ago, we didn't listen to God when we were in our own land. The prophets told our ancestors to follow God's laws, but they didn't. Because of that, God was very upset with the Jews.

He pulled His protectiveness away from us, and that's why the Babylonians came and took the Israelites captive to this place, Babylon. But we're still Jews, and one day soon, God will allow us to go back home. That's what I learned from Teacher Azariah.

That's why it's really important for us to learn the Torah and understand God's laws. You need to go to classes, Zaccai, and learn about our God and our people. Please ask your father again—it's very important.

Zaccai sat with his head in his hands, then he jumped up. "Come, let's play skipping stones," he yelled and ran away. Nebo chased him and soon enough they were in heavy competitions. They skipped stones over the river and Zaccai jumped around, throwing his hands in the air and laughing when he won.

"This place is much better than where we lived when we were in the Babylonian city, Kish," said Nebo laughing. "I love the river of Kibar! How much fun is it to be here! In Kish we were much poorer and we lived in a very small home, but here we have all this space by the river to run and play."

"I was raised here in Nippur," said Zaccai. My father has worked for the King since he was 12 years old and my grandfather worked in the palace since they came to this country. We have always had a big house and I love this river!"

"You are lucky," Nebo said. "Most of our family works very hard in the fields to produce the food for all the people. They don't have a choice like your father and my father have." Nebo paused then suddenly remembered he needed to get home. "Hey, I need to go home. A runner arrived yesterday to announce that an important visitor, brother Zerubbabel, will come tonight to visit my father and talk about a new decree the King has ushered."

"Who is he?" asked Zaccai, "another priest?" "No, he works for the King, and he's coming to speak with my father and I hope my father will let me stay in the conversation. I am almost a man you know!"

Together the two friends hurried back not knowing that this was the day their lives would be changed forever.

CHAPTER 2

The Decree

Nebo's Mother, "Child hurry and wash your hands. You cannot come to the table unclean. Do you want to bring shame on your father? In these trying times? Who knows what the King has planned now," She said.

Nebo silently wondered what it could be. Would it be something good for the jews?

Or were they bringing harsher laws?

"Here here," said Ah-Bee and patted his wife Ima on her back. "It will not be so bad, I think. We have been doing well in this country. We never give the King any problems. And we pay taxes. So, I don't think we will be in trouble."

"Well, I don't know!" said Ima with trembling hands. "First, they come in our country and steal the people and the flocks. Then they bring us to this country and make us live and work for them. We cannot go to our own country. When will we be able to worship our God in our own Temple?"

"We just need to be patient," said Ah-bee. "Remember, Jeremiah prophesied that the Lord will eventually forgive us and let us go back? Maybe it is that time."

Nebo jumped up when he heard that. "Do you think that Ah-bee?" he asked his father with big eyes. "Do you think we are going back?"

"I don't know son," said his father while he ruffled Nebo's hair. "But I will not be surprised if it was. We have been praying so long for this to happen. I know what Jeremiah said. Remember I made you memorize this when you were six years old?"

"Yes Ah-bee, I know," said Nebo and stood tall to recite the words of the prophet Jeremiah.

> *"Change your lives and stop*
> *doing evil! If you change,*
> *you can return to the land*

that the Lord gave you and your ancestors long ago. He gave you this land to live in forever. Don't follow other gods. Don't serve or worship them. Don't worship idols that someone has made. That only makes me angry with you. By doing this you only hurt yourselves."

His father beamed with pride in his son.

That very night Zerubbabel arrived, tired and dusty from the long travels. He used water to wash himself before sitting down to eat. Friends I bring news from the King," he said. "The King has ushered a new decree. I would like you to

travel to the city of Babylon with me. There is much work to be done. Can you do that?" Brother Zerubbabel asked.

Ah-bee nodded slowly. Then he turned to Nebo and said, "You run along now Nebo, go to your mother as I talk with our brother Zerubbabel."

"But Ah-bee!" said Nebo, and hung his head. "I was hoping...that...that...I could stay now...to

hear...since I am sitting at the feet of Teacher Azariah. I am almost a man," he said proudly.

Ah-bee smiled. "Only if you can be as still as a mouse," he said. "If I hear you even breathing, you will go to the kitchen to help your mother!"

"I will be so still...you will even forget I am in this corner," said Nebo laughing and he curled in the corner with some scrolls that he was using to scribe his Hebrew text. He planned to take notes of the conversation so he could practice his Hebrew.

Ima came in with the usual cordialities of sweet milk and date cookies that she had prepared. Then Brother Zerubbabel told them his news.

Nebo, filled with excitement from what he was hearing, could not keep quiet anymore. He actually jumped up, screamed, and stared at brother Zerubbabel with open mouth.

Thankfully Ah-bee hadn't noticed that Nebo stood there. Quickly Nebo lowered himself in his corner and started writing. Nebo noticed Ah-bee's open mouth too.

"Brother Zerubbabel, is this true?" Ah-bee asked while he was twisting his long beard with his fingers, like he does when he is without words. The news brother Zerubbabel brought was indeed a big surprise.

"The king, yes, the king himself, had ordered a decree on behalf of the Jewish people. They are free to go back to their country!" Brother Zerubbabel said. "And that is not all. The King ordered to give the Jewish people bags of gold and silver, as much money as they needed to

rebuild the temple! Also, the King decided to give back all the precious bowls, plates, ornaments and pots that were stolen from the temple in the time of the former king Nebuchadnezzar."

All this good news seemed too good to be true. But it was true.

Brother Zerubbabel showed Ah-bee a scroll and began reading the letter that the King had written. Nebo wrote it all down, word for word.

This is what King Cyrus of Persia says:

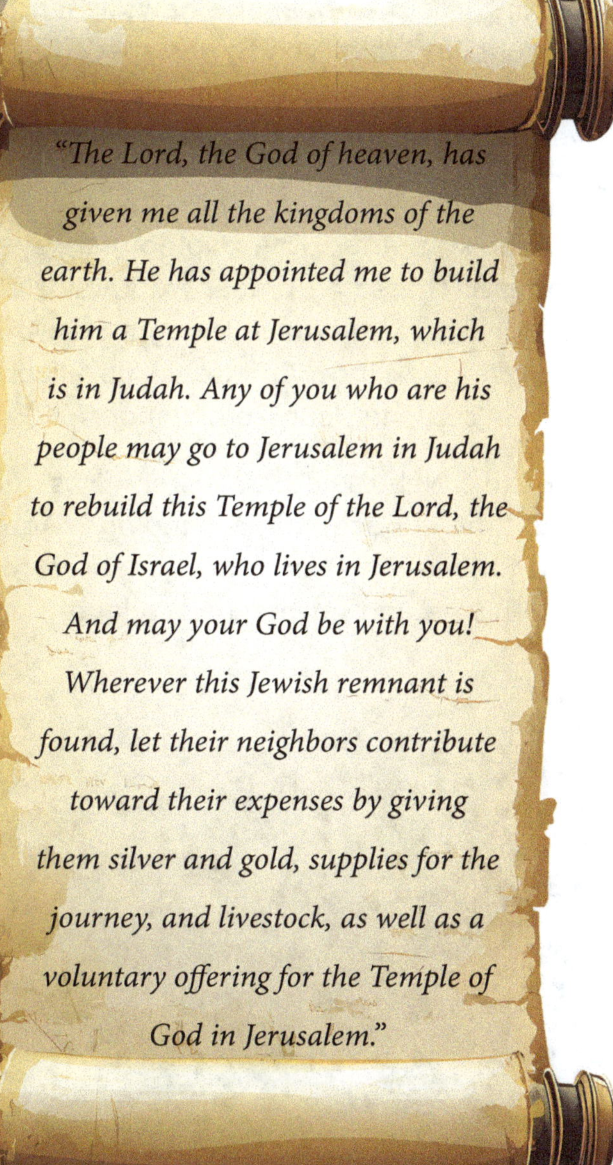

That night nobody slept. Ah-bee forgot to send Nebo to bed. Nebo's two sisters came into the sitting room to hear the news when brother Zerubbabel left. Everybody was speechless. Inai, Nebo's oldest sister, cried a little. She felt sad to leave the only country she had ever known. She had many friends in this city.

Nebo's mother was wiping her eyes and laughing at the same time. "We knew He would do it, but who would have thought He would use a king? A real king? And...give us all our gold back? Isn't Adonai, our God, wonderful?"

Bilah, Nebo's other sister, was dancing around the house while singing "Adonai is wonderful, his love for Israel endures forever." And both Ima and Ah-bee had to laugh.

Nebo quietly refilled the oil in the lamps since he saw that they were getting too low. He was tired after a long night of talking.

The next day the news spread through the whole city and many came to Nebo's father to ask for prayers and advice. As long as Nebo remained quiet, Ah-bee left him in his corner with his scrolls.

Nebo made a list of everything that was going on. He was very proud of himself. He wrote down the names of the people who would be going, how many children they had, what they wanted to do in Judah, among other things. When Zaccai came over, Nebo showed Zaccai his private scrolls and translated them for him. Zaccai had heard the news too. "I'm sure my father doesn't want to go," Zaccai said that morning while they were skipping stones on the river.

"You don't mean that," said Nebo with big eyes. "Adonai did this for us! He even used a king and gave us gold and silver and animals to bring back. How can you want to stay?"

"My father says that it is crazy to go back. It is a dream he says. Jerusalem is only rubbles. There are no roads, no homes, no stores, no jobs. What are we going to do there? Just build a temple and worship God? And what are we going to eat?

My father says that Adonai has provided for us right here in Babylon so we should be thankful for that and enjoy it instead of running after the dream of our forefathers." Zaccai spoke earnestly as if he was trying to convince Nebo, but Nebo clasped his hands over his ears as he didn't want to hear anymore.

He said, "Our God, Adonai, is always faithful. I learned in class that God spoke to the people of Judah through special men called prophets. These prophets told everyone to do the right thing, but most didn't listen.

Because they didn't listen, God took His protection away. That's why the Babylonians were able to come and take us away to this country. That's why we are living far from our home now."

Zaccai shook his head. "If Adonai wanted us to be in Judah, He would have protected us there. God wants us here! Don't you see Nebo? God just used the Babylonians to bring us here. We have nice big houses here. We eat meat. We have all we need here. Why go back? We don't even speak the language anymore."

Nebo pleaded with Zaccai. "Zaccai, open your eyes and see. God punished the Babylonians for doing that with our forefathers. Look where they are now! The Persians have taken them over; they lost all their power and now the king the king of the Persians wants to help the Jewish people. And we can go back! Don't you see God's hand in this plan?" "I really don't know Nebo," said Zaccai with his head hanging. "I am only telling you what my father is saying. Your father is a priest, he is poor already, so he can go to Israel but my father is rich. He will become poor if he goes and he doesn't want that. I think you will be leaving and I will stay here with my father."

That day the best friends left each other without the normal laughter and banter. Each went quietly to their own homes.

Nebo sat in the corner and listened to the people talking with his father. To his surprise, he heard more people with the same arguments as Zaccai. But his father was much better at explaining the Word of God to them. He encouraged all the men to take their families and go with Zerubbabel to Israel.

Not only was the situation tense between Nebo and Zaccai, but also between Ima and Ahbee. Nebo noticed very well Ima's red eyes and puffy cheeks. She didn't say anything to Nebo and he didn't want to ask. He went to the kitchen twice that afternoon and was extra nice to Ima, helping her fetch water from the river to wash some floors and being of help in the shed. Ima didn't say too much.

Later Bilah explained the situation to Nebo. "It is because of Grandpa Saba that Ima is worried," she said. "He is too old to travel and Ima doesn't want to leave him alone without family in Babylon." "Oh my...I forgot all about Saba. And he has been sick these days. He has a nagging cough and weak bones. He can't travel like that," said Nebo.

"Ah-bee didn't want to hear about staying behind for Saba's sake," said Bilah, "and that is why Ima is sad."

That night they spoke about the problem at the dinner table. Ah-bee was curling his beard again and everyone could see that he was not

comfortable with what he had to say.

"Ima, I know it is tough but how can we disobey God? How can we stay in this country just because your father is too old to travel? What would Adonai have to say about that?" he asked.

"Didn't Adonai say to Moses in the 10 commandments to honor your father and mother? How would it be honoring them if I leave this country and leave him to die? Alone?" Ima said, pleading with Ah-bee.

"Ima!" Nebo with his eyes wide open. "Is Saba going to die?"

"No Nebo, he will not. But I think you all need to go to Jerusalem without me. I will stay behind and take care of him and when his time comes to be with the Lord, I will find transportation and follow you," said Ima.

Nebo jumped up from his reclining position. "Ima, No! We can't go without…you," Ah-bee said, part statement and part question.

Bilah and Inai were already crying and Ah-bee curled his beard more. Nobody could eat. They had a real dilemma on their hands.

"Ima," Ah-bee said sternly. "I can't leave you behind. Who is going to take care of you? Where will you get food? I will not be making money in Israel. I will be the priest and we will get food from the temple but if I leave you here who will protect you? You belong with your family, your husband and kids. You are coming with me. Let's go sleep and we will pray more about this and see how Adonai is going to help us, as he has always done. We are not leaving tomorrow so there is time to pray."

The next day, Nebo told Zaccai exchanged stories about what had been happening in their homes.

Zaccai was very distracted and the usual games didn't go well. Finally he went to sit under a tree of figs and ate some. Nebo sat next to him on a stone. Nobody spoke at first.

Then Zaccai said. "I asked my father to let me use some of my time to learn to write Hebrew with teacher Azariah. It will be good for my education to know more languages, especially if many Jews are going back because they will need documents in Hebrew now."

"Ai, Zaccai that is good news! You will see. When teacher Azariah explains the law to you, it all will make much more sense," said Nebo. The next day, Zaccai, staying true to his words, came by to pick up Nebo for classes with Azariah.

He was a quick student having picked up lots of Hebrew from Ah-bee and Ima when he came to visit. They insisted on speaking the Old

Language in the house. Azariah turned out to be a fantastic teacher of the Law. He could recite the whole Law of Moses and had answers for all the curious boys' questions. His goal was for the boys to learn that too. He became a very good friend to Zaccai and Nebo.

CHAPTER 3

Preparations for the Journey

During the time of quiet preparation for their journey to Jerusalum, Zerubbabel came back on two occasions to talk with Ah-bee. On one of those visits, Ah-bee left with Zerubbabel to go speak with Jeshua, the high priest and the leader of the first group that was to depart for Jerusalem. Jeshua and Zerubbabel were planning to take as many people as possible to Jerusalem. They had to prepare for the entire journey and organize all the details. First, they traveled to the country provinces to tell about the decree and to encourage people to sign up for the move back home. This took up most of the year. Later Ah-bee was asked to go with them to some larger cities like the large commercial cities of Nippur, Niniveh, Babylon and Gozan. This trip would take most of a year too and Nebo's family was sad to see Ah-bee leave.

Then one Monday morning, both Nebo and Zaccai stood at the shore of Kebar as Ah-bee was preparing to take a small boat to his first stop, the city of Calah. Nebo kept holding on to Ah-bee and hugging him while Ah-bee was trying to get his belongings into the boat. "I wish I could go with you Ah-bee," he kept saying.

"I know," said Ah-bee, "and I wish you could too, but you have to finish the classes with teacher Azariah before we leave for Israel. And I might be gone now for many months, maybe a year."

Nebo grabbed Ah-bee again and gave him a big hug. "I will do my best and learn the law as much as possible from teacher Azariah," he promised with a gruff voice.

"That's my boy," said Ah-bee as he grabbed his last bag of scrolls and flipped it in the boat. "I would not have enough time to teach you now that I'm traveling. Also, you need to take care of Ima, Bilah and Inai; you are the man of the house now. Don't forget that."

Nebo beamed. "Did you hear that?" he asked Zaccai over and over again as they walked home. "Ah-bee said that I'm the man of the house now."

From that day on, Nebo took his job seriously. He helped Ima with all the heavy work in the house: carrying water, chopping wood and keeping the fires going. Zaccai turned out to be a good friend in these days too. He never insisted on playtime at the riverbank like they used to do, he helped with the chores in the house, and they invented new games around the house. It was like they were much more grown up now that the time of leaving came closer. They were almost 11 now and had learned to shoulder work.

Saba, Nebo's grandpa came to stay with them. He was still very sick and coughed and gasped as he laid on his mat. Nebo helped Ima give him his poultices to get rid of the flu. He even learned how to make the poultice for Saba using flour, mixed with dry mustard seed and water. He applied this to the chest of Saba, then waited until it was dry before removing it and applying another one to Saba's back. This should help Saba with his coughing, chest congestion and croup. But very soon after the poultice, Saba was coughing again.

"Oh Saba, can't you eat a little so you can get better?" Nebo asked while he tried to feed Saba a spoon of lentil soup. But Saba was coughing and pushed him away. "Sorry son," he managed to say and laid down again, coughing.

"Ima, we need to buy Saba some medicine.

He is not getting better," said Nebo.

"I was thinking the same," said Ima as she wiped her eyes. "I will go in the morning to the finance house Mashur in the city to talk with him about extra money. Ah-bee left instructions with him."

"I want you to sell something for me too," gasped Saba with a very hoarse voice. "Nebo look in my box and you will find some property scrolls. I want to sell all of them."

Nebo read over them and showed them to Ima. "Are you sure Saba?" asked Ima. "These are most of your properties your land, your house, and some patches of land here in Nipur."

After a long haul of coughing, Saba managed to say "Do it, I don't need them anymore. You can put the money to better use in Jerusalem."

The very next morning Ima asked Nebo to join her on her journey to the financial district.

Ima and Nebo both took a donkey and carried food for the way. It was the first time Nebo would go to the financial district. And now he's doing it as head of the family. "Oh Ima look at all these big buildings." Nebo couldn't sit still on his donkey. He kept pointing to one building and then the other.

Finally they arrived at the financial house of Mashur. A scribe from the family aproached them. They explained the situation about the money and asked the scribe to sell the properties that Saba identified. The scribe took the scroll and scribbled something in a language that Nebo thought he recognized but did not speak or write. It was not Aramaic for sure. Nebo thought it could have been Cuneiform. The scribe wrote

down some mathematic problems and then gave Ima some gold coins. He promised to settle the rest with Ah-bee upon his return.

Nebo didn't have to speak at all. It went quickly and satisfactorily.

Ima went to the market and bought what she needed while Nebo carried it home for her. Later that day some of the neighbor women came to visit Ima, and Nebo left to play with Zaccai. When he returned, he heard Ima and Saba talking and Ima sounded upset.

He looked for his sister and asked "Bilah what happened? Why is Ima upset?"

"The women who came to visit wanted to pray to their god En-lil for Saba. And they wanted to make offerings on his behalf," said Bilah in a hushed voice.

"And what did Saba do?" asked Nebo.

Bilah held her hands in front of her mouth to hide a laugh and said, "He told them that he'd rather die than follow their god. They left hurriedly and not in a good mood."

Nebo snickered too. That's just what Saba would say. He shook his head. "So many people serving the god En-lil. They truly believe he is the father of all other gods. Even kings come to sacrifice for him," he told Bilah who listened with big ears.

"Nebo, you know so much!" she said and she was proud of him.

"I learned that from my teacher," he said and went to find his mother.

Nebo, Ima and grandfather prayed together and used the new medicine. The medicine seemed to work because the very next day Saba could sit up, and two weeks later he felt much better and was able to walk around the house. However, it took him longer than three months to fully recover and start sharing in chores again. Still there was no sign of Ah-bee and everybody missed him a lot. Especially Nebo.

To be honest, Nebo didn't like the part of being the man of the house too much. He was secretly happy that Saba stayed with them and helped him shoulder the load. That freed him up to be able to go for long walks and play games with Zaccai.

Zaccai stayed for dinner many times and they all spoke Hebrew together. After dinner they played a board game with Saba who turned out to be a good craftsman. He crafted all the small pieces for the game, out of stone. During the game, the conversation turned to leaving Babylon for Israel.

"Are you already preparing for the big trip?" Saba asked Zaccai. For a moment it was completely still around the table. Nebo had forgotten that Saba didn't know about Zaccai not leaving. Saba was too sick when he arrived in their household to understand what was going on.

Nobody responded and Saba looked from one to the other.

Nebo tried to say something, "Ehhh...the thing is...ehhh...well..."

Ima wanted to say something too but couldn't find the words. "Anybody want a date cookie?" she ended up asking. But nobody answered.

Finally Zaccai said "I'm not leaving, Saba. My dad wants us all to stay in this country."

"What??" exclaimed Saba. "Young man", he said with his thunder voice. "Adonai wants us to go back! It is our Promised Land. Why would you want to stay in this country? We are all going back."

Zaccai, who was sitting on the floor and dipping some bread into a thick soup, felt very uneasy. He continued dipping the bread but he never ate it. "But Saba, surely you can't go back either. You have been sick. The trip back is going to be very long and dangerous," said Zaccai.

Nebo held his breath. Until now, nobody had dared to open the topic, but Zaccai just did.

"I am certainly going back!" shouted Saba. "I'd rather die on the road trying to get back than stay here and die in disobedience to the Lord. I will go back."

"But Saba..." said Nebo with a small trembling voice. "We need to walk for many days. Maybe three or four months or more. How can you do that? Even when you walk around the house you are out of breath."

"Yes Saba," said Bilah with her small sweet voice. "We better stay here in Babylon with you. The road back is too hard for you."

"Look here," boomed Saba. "I am a grown man and I've made my decision. I will go to my land. God will help me reach it and if I need to die on the road, just bury me anywhere and leave me there. I will be with God and in God's will. That is what counts."

The family talked long with Saba, discussing many scenarios on how to get to Jerusalem, but they were unable to make a good plan. Saba was determined; he was going to Israel. That much was clear.

Later that evening, everybody rolled out their sleeping mats and got comfortable for the night.

The next morning they had the surprise of their life!

Ah-bee sat on the low table when they woke up! "Ah-bee!!!!" Everybody rushed over to hug him and Bilah kept pulling on his beard and hair. Both had grown more since he left.

He looked thin and tired but he assured Ima that it was because of the trip. "I missed your good cooking." He laughed and put a big piece of the date pancake Ima made in his mouth.

Saba joined Ah-bee at the table and began speaking right away.

"Son," he said, "I am going to Israel with you when you go. I am not staying behind. I made a plan last night. While you were gone, I sold a piece of my land to buy what I needed to recover from the cold. Musher has the rest of the money and we should go there to finish our financial business. But I have more to sell. I will

sell my small house and the rest of the land. With that money I will buy a donkey to carry me and a donkey to carry my possessions that I want to bring. I will also hire two strong, young men from Babylon who would like to travel with us to carry me and to help me. So I will not be a burden for you. I have it all planned out."

Ah-bee was certainly taken aback by the faith of Saba. It was obvious that Saba had spent a lot of time thinking and planning, and Ah-bee agreed to help him sell his possessions and buy what he needed.

Ima was crying again but this time from happiness. Nebo was sure about that.

Now that Ah-bee had returned, the departure date had been set and was approaching quickly.

Many people went to Mashur to try to sell their possessions. Some could sell easily and some couldn't. Ah-bee could. Their house was just in the middle of the commercial district and close to the market. Many people were interested and Ah-bee sold it quickly. He bought donkeys for both his family and Saba. Then he bought cows, goats and many more things they needed for the trip, the temple and to start a new life. All the travelers wanted camels so it was difficult to find camels, but Ah-bee managed to get four and brought them home with him.

CHAPTER 4

The Journey Comes Closer

Zaccai came every day to help out. He was changed. He prayed to Adonai now all the time and he loved to study the scrolls with Azariah. He was dreading Azariah's leaving just as he was dreading Nebo's.

Then one day they all got some astonishing news. They learned that Azariah would not be leaving. He was asked to stay behind to guide the group of Jewish people who weren't going back but still needed to know and practice the law. For Zaccai, this was good news, but for Nebo it came as a total shock. His good friend and teacher would stay behind. But thinking of his friend, he said, "I am happy you can continue to study with Azariah." He smiled encouragingly to his friend. "Keep praying. Maybe your father will change his mind when Azariah has the chance to come, and then you can come with him. I will wait for you in Jerusalem."

Zaccai promised to come with Azariah and to meet Nebo in Jerusalem.

Finally the day of leaving arrived. Many families reunited on the square in the middle of the town. Neighbors came to say goodbye and many brought bags full of gold, silver and food to give to the Jews. It was a joyous but sad day.

Zaccai stood with his head down. He had just said his goodbyes to most of his family. All his cousins, aunts and uncles were leaving. Even his grandfather had made preparation to leave. And his best friend Nebo. He felt as if he were the only one staying behind.

Nebo saw Zaccai standing alone and he came to be with him. "Don't be sad, Zaccai," he said. "Soon you can come with your teacher or maybe another caravan. Your father might change his mind."

"You are right," said Zaccai, "let's go over to your family to say goodbye. I have many gifts for you all."

Zaccai's father was talking and hugging Nebo's family tight. Zaccai was handing out presents. Zaccai gave Ima many golden bangles for her arms and even Nebo's sisters got some. He gave Nebo a scroll with the copied words of the Law in Hebrew. He had made it himself. He also brought six cows, 12 goats, date cake and dried fruits for Nebo. "Zaccai, this is too much. Is this ok with your parents?" Ah-bee asked him.

"We have more than enough," said Zaccai. My father will not even miss this but I have his permission to give it to you. Go with peace. SHALOM," and he grinned.

Zaccai helped Nebo take the animals to his flock and store the presents. It was their last day together and neither of them knew what to say.

"Have you seen Ah-bee?" Ima, out of breath, called to Nebo. "Go look for him and tell him that he is needed. They want him to count the golden items that the King is sending back for the Temple of God. He needs to go to the front of the caravan."

Zaccai and Nebo made their way through the throngs of people looking for Ah-bee. At the edge of the square they found him in the middle of a heated discussion.

"What is going on?" Zaccai pointed to Ah-bee and Nebo saw him too. Slowly they came closer to hear. Ah-bee was curling his beard and was trying to be heard while another Jewish man was flapping his hands in the air and talking fast.

"Hobaiah," said Ah-bee in a reasonable tone of voice. "We cannot decide that matter now. You cannot prove from which family you come. You can't find your family in the records. So I can't know it. Why don't we leave this matter for Jerusalem?"

"I am a priest!" said the man Ah-bee called Hobaiah. "I know I am a priest. How can you not believe me?"

"Hobaiah, it is not a matter of not believing you. You just cannot prove it and I can't record you as such. That is why the governor has told you not to eat from the priest's share of food. If you want to let this matter rest then I promise you that we will consult the Lord as soon as we arrive in Jerusalem using Urim and Thummin." Ah-bee's voice was soothing but also commanding and Hobaiah calmed down a little.

"Oh, exciting," said Nebo to Zaccai. "The Urim and Thummin are the sacred lots.

When the priest doesn't have the answers, they ask God and throw the lots. That is how God talks to them."

"Oh that is exciting," said Zaccai. They waited until they saw a chance to push forward to get Ah-bee's attention.

"Ah-bee," said Nebo as he pulled his father's hand. "The leaders need you to count the gold for the temple. Can you go to the front of the line?"

Ah-bee gave Hobaiah a hand and they all walked together to their families. Ah-bee talked with Zaccai's father for a minute and left quickly for the front of the line.

Zaccai's father was leading a heavy-loaded donkey when he saw Nebo and called out to him. "Nebo, here! I was looking for you. I brought you something." Nebo walked slowly to Zaccai's father. "I already got a present from Zaccai," he said slowly. "I know but my wife and I are very thankful for your friendship with Zaccai and we wanted to give you something you will need in the new country. Here you go," he said as he placed the donkey's reins in Nebo's hand.

Nebo looked the heavy-laden donkey over.

Many packages where tied to the animal and he was wearing a fine handmade blanket over his back. "For me?" Nebo asked. "We have many donkeys with us for carrying people and their things."

"I know", said Zaccai laughing, but this one is a special donkey. "You need to keep this one too. It is for helping you get started in Jerusalem." Zaccai opened one of the packages tied to the donkey and Nebo saw layers and layers of empty scrolls. "And look," said Zaccai, "here is the clay to make seals and tablets, and also some pens for writing. You have all you need here to become a great scribe. Please use this to record all the things you experience from the long trip and from the building of the Temple. Then one day I hope I can read what you wrote and it will be as if I was there." Zaccai was beaming with his plan and Nebo caught his fire too.

"Thank you so very much!" he said glowing and he gave Zaccai's father a hug and Zaccai an extra tight bear hug.

At that very moment, the singers elevated their voices and the trumpet sounded, indicating the start of the march.

Slowly the group began walking and forming the caravan. Families walked together, bringing with them all their flocks, and leading their donkeys which had been loaded down with possessions. The young men grouped around the animals to protect them from wandering off or being stolen by thieves on the road. Some older and sick people were sitting on donkeys, while others were carried by families on hand-made carriers.

The Kings' soldiers were walking at the front and the end of the caravan and some patrolled the sides. They were on leggy horses and looked terrifying to the people, but they also gave the people a sense of protection.

Meanwhile the singers were singing verses from the scrolls of Isaiah saying:

"The wilderness and the desert will be glad, encourage the exhausted, and strengthen the feeble. Say to those with anxious heart, a highway will be there, a roadway, and it will be called the Highway of Holiness. The unclean will not travel on it, but it will be for him who walks that way, and fools will not wander on it. No lion will be there, nor will any vicious beast go up on it; these will not be found there. But the redeemed will walk there, and the ransomed of the Lord will return and come with joyful shouting to Zion, with everlasting joy upon their heads."

CHAPTER 5

The Highway

A new adventure had started for Nebo. He was on the new Highway. He was going home. The home his heavenly father had planned for him. He waved to Zaccai, his great friend, as long as he could see him. That was difficult because his eyes were full of water (from the dust, of course, not from anything else).

That first day on the road was exciting. Everybody was joyful, patting each other on the shoulders, laughing and praising the Lord. Most of the older people sat on donkeys and were talking to each other. The large group formed a colorful

caravan heading West. They moved at a quicker pace than the leaders had predicted. The little children ran along and covered about three times the distance the adults did. Nobody felt tired. Nobody was complaining. They followed the river and had a continual supply of fresh water.

Just before dark they broke for the day and made up their camp. The men assembled the makeshift tents and the women made fire with the wood that the kids had gathered. Ima had a small feast planned. She was baking bread, as well as some soup with dumplings. She was also cooking beans, out of which she planned to make hummus to go with the bread. Some of the other families came to sit with Ah-bee and they also brought food so they could all eat together. It tasted good. Nebo played and talked with many of his cousins, some of which he hadn't seen in quite some time. Now was a good time to catch up.

"So glad I can sit down," said Nebo, as he took his place next to cousin Bani. "I'm dead tired." He inspected his feet and his cousin did the same. "My feet sure feel like clay blocks," Nebo said.

"Let's go sit on the bank of the river," Bani said, "then we can dangle our feet in the fresh water and cool down."

Nebo didn't feel like walking anymore but he managed to arrive to the river. The minute he sat down in the cool grass, he was glad he did. "Ahhhh, this is better, I'm going try to take a swim tomorrow. It is too dark now." His cousin agreed. The boys enjoyed relaxing and soaking their feet as they told stories and made plans for their arrival in Jerusalem.

Just a short time later, Ah-bee called the young people to open their mats and go to bed. They did as they were told and enjoyed a restful night.

Early the next day they fixed breakfast again. Ima and the girls made flatbreads to be eaten with some of the leftover hummus. It tasted heavenly for Nebo, especially when he added some slices of onions and leek that Ima gave him. After the morning rituals, it was time to pack up and start a day of walking. The going was hard. It was hot and Nebo's back was aching from the weight of the load he had been carrying. Finally, he managed to make some space on his donkey and tie his sachet on its back, which gave him some much-needed relief.

The caravan moved until the sun was at its highest point, and then the signal came to take a break. Relieved, Nebo sat down next to Bilah. He looked at his sister's feet and flinched. They were red and blistered. "Oh sis," he said, "I am sorry."

He jumped back up, returned to his sachet and looked through it until he found some older tallit katans (underskirts Jewish boys wear). Each morning, by prayer time, he was supposed to put one of his tallit katans under his tunic. He had just received new tallit katans for the new life in Jerusalem, so he took one of his old ones and asked God for forgiveness before ripping it to shreds and dipping the pieces in the river. Then he bowed down before his sister Bilah and cleaned her feet with the wet material. Ima gave him some olive oil, which he used to rub Bilah's feet before bandaging them with the rest of the shreds. Some of the color returned to Bilah's face and she smiled thankfully at him.

After everyone had a chance to drink a little and rest their bodies, the caravan took off again.

Nebo decided to carry his pouch again. He made a space for his sister to sit on one of the donkeys and made a space for his mother too. He knew she would never complain but if he himself was so tired, how much more tired would she be?

Again the large caravan started moving and followed the route. The dust of the people before them penetrated their noses and Nebo used more of his tallit katans to make some mouth and nose coverings for him and his family. The group didn't move as quickly as it did the day before. Children didn't run along as much anymore and the older people were limping. But nobody complained. They kept on walking. It was still far off to Jerusalem.

That night, they broke early for camp and made dinner. Nebo got a chance to get in the water before it was dark and many other boys followed. The girls and the women went upstream and lowered themselves in the water too; some of them fully clothed. It felt so good to remove the road's dust from their bodies.

Some of the boys went fishing and Nebo followed them. He managed to bring home two fish and Ima made a delicious soup.

For the next three days the group traveled at this slow tempo and soon their strength began to return. Their feet were stronger, the blisters of the first days were healed, and the resulting callouses were helping lessen their pain. The caravan was underway from sun up to sun down. Along the way, as their food supply began to shrink, they had to start looking for food. They still had beans and roots and enough grain in the packages and bags, but Ima wanted to be careful with portion sizes because she didn't   know when they would find new foods to eat. To her delight though, they found many pomegranate trees with ripe fruits along the way and all the kids filled their bellies. In a matter of hours, the people had stripped all the trees of the ripe fruits and packed them to take along, giving thanks for the provision of the Lord. The same happened a week later but this time they found fig trees.

Nebo kept fishing and brought home many fish, which they either ate right away or smoked so they could carry them along to eat later. On Friday they had to cook enough food for two days in order to keep the Sabbath. The caravan stopped early and Ah-bee went to fish with Nebo. It was a fun time. When Ah-bee waded out in the river to retrieve a fish, Nebo gave him a hard push and Ah-bee tumbled, but before he fell, he grasped Nebo's tunic and they both fell into the river. "Got ya!" Ah-bee shouted and Nebo cried out when his body hit the cold water. "That is why you should never try to outsmart a priest," he gasped and they both laughed. Thankfully, even after their playful moment, the fish was still there and they pulled it out. They had enough food for their dinner and for the next day as well. Ima decided to smoke the fish. Smoking fish took a long time, but since no one was in a hurry, she made a smoky fire and began the process. Meanwhile, Nebo changed his tunic and set the wet one out to dry.

Later that night, Ah-bee assembled all the men and their families and they said their evening's prayers. Ah-bee read the word of God, and it was a nice, quiet time for all. Ima made a hot beverage and sweetened it with honey. Some of the men missed the beer they used to drink in Babylon, but Ah-bee made sure to explain that drinking alcohol was not to be done by the followers of Adonai and for now, it appeared that the men agreed.

The next day was the Sabbath and the priests gathered and held a public scripture reading that took most of the morning. Men, women and children worshipped God and shouted praises. For the remainder of the day, everyone rested and held small, quiet talks in their tents.

This is the routine they followed for much of the next several weeks.

By their third week of travel, most people felt like expert nomads. They kept to their routines and walked most of the days. Nobody became sick or suffered major injuries, and for that, they continuously sang praise to the Lord.

In the fourth week, two memorable things happened. First, though it was completely unexpected, a pregnant woman suddenly had to give birth. They made a make-shift carrier for the expectant mother and carried her most of the

day. When the baby was due to arrive, they made camp early and some of the women carried the pregnant sister into some bushes. They stayed with her until the next day when they came out with a smiling mother and a small baby. He was named Ebenezer, "until here the Lord has helped me," she said, smiling and showing her baby to the people.

"Born on the highway back to our Promised Land," the father said proudly and smiled. The caravan stayed an extra day at the camping place to rest. The people used the time to wash and dry some of their clothes and to bake cookies or dried fish. It felt like a holiday to them.

CHAPTER 6

Robbers in the Night

The second unexpected thing to occur happened that night while Nebo was in a deep sleep. Suddenly, he heard shouting voices and running. When Nebo sat up, Ah-bee was already throwing some clothes on and Nebo followed hurriedly.

"What is going on?" Ah-bee asked even though he didn't expect an answer from Nebo. Quickly they pushed the flap of the tent open and stepped into the dark night. In the soft moonlight they could see a group of men talking and yelling to each other. When they came closer, Nebo heard one of the men say "We need to follow them! I want my donkeys back. How am I going to bring my father in law to Jerusalem without a donkey?"

"Let's wait for the leaders to come," another man said. "Bani already went to call Zerubbabel and Jeshua," then turning to Ah-bee he said, "and here is our teacher already." It turned out that thieves had attacked the camp and stolen some of the cows and the donkeys. Thankfully, it was nighttime so the donkeys didn't have the group's priceless possessions strapped to them, but they were still necessary for the transportation of people and goods.

The soldier on watch was found beaten and gagged in the bushes. The other soldiers rapidly

formed a barrier around the caravan to protect them from more calamities. Ah-bee roused more men and they prayed together. They decided to go after the animals so Zerubbabel quickly organized a search committee.

"Ah-bee can I go too?" begged Nebo, jumping from one leg to the other. "Pleeeaase."

But Ah-bee didn't want to let him come. "No, Nebo, this is going to be dangerous enough. Those thieves attacked a soldier!"

"Oh please, please Ah-bee. How many times have I helped out on the farms? I know how to follow the tracks of animals and I have good eyes; I can be of great help."

When Ah-bee saw that the other families let their young boys go, he nodded 'yes' and Nebo ran to his tent to tell his mother the news.

Some of the men were dipping their handmade torches in grease to light them for the dark route. Other men found rope and swords to bring with them. In a hurry, the group left in the direction that the soldier had indicated.

"It is so dark," said Nebo.

"If not for the torches we wouldn't be able to see anything," said Ah-bee. They kept the torches very low to the ground. They didn't want the light to show and tip off the thieves. With the torches low they could see the tracks and broken leaves where the animals had been.

"Move slowly," said Ah-bee "and don't make any noise." Light footed and in a quick march, the men moved forward. The path the thieves took was easy to follow. Nobody had made any attempt to cover it up.

Nebo's eyes adjusted to the darkness and he could see more easily. Maybe it was because of the soft light given off by the moon, or maybe he was now just used to the dark. The other men were also adjusting to the dark, and because they didn't want to give themselves away with too much light, some of them extinguished their torches.

After two hours of walking, they heard the bleating of a cow in distress. Quickly the men put out most of the torches. Bani and his other cousin, Akan, volunteered to stay behind with one burning torch to keep the fire going. The rest of the men, as well as Nebo, slowly and cautiously followed the noise of the cow. Quietly, they moved forward in a bent position. Nebo's felt his heart beating in his throat. He grasped Ah-bee's hand as they came upon a small camp. Six men sat around a small fire, drinking and laughing. They surely didn't expect to be followed. Nebo could smell them from far away. One of the men stood up and went to tie the cow. He appeared to have trouble with the cow, as it didn't want to stay put. Nebo knew why! The cow had a young but the thieves had not brought her calf along. "That cow was not going to be an easy one," Nebo thought to himself and snickered. "Not too smart with animals now are you?"

They came very close to the thieves' camp.

They had a small fire burning that gave just enough light to see two men get up and attempt to calm down the distressed cow.

They were rough-looking robbers. Their dirty clothes hung on their skinny bodies, and their long hair, bound together ponytails, looked particularly greasy.

Ah-bee signaled to Nebo to stand back and he himself tiptoed to the leaders. None of them knew what to do or how to proceed. They were not really prepared to fight and the robbers with their swords looked dangerous to them. Ah-bee prayed. Nebo and his friends bowed their heads and prayed too.

Suddenly the mother cow went silent and an eerie sound pierced the quiet of the night. Nebo's hair stood on end and he prayed harder. "What was that?" he thought. Two of his cousins grasped his hands and they stood there in quiet prayers, waiting to see what was going to happen.

Again the sound pierced the air, only this time much closer. It sounded like a small thunder mixed with an eerie voice, whispering something from far away.

"Don't panic," said Nebo to his cousins. "I think it is the wind. Adonai is scaring them off with the wind." As soon as he said that, the robbers began running around, picking up their things, and packing their bags in a hurry. They were so frantic that they bumped into each other and pushed each other. Their voices were now clearly audible because the cow had stopped making noise. Nebo was familiar with the dialect and recognized it to be of the people of the North. He had heard it many times when they came to do business in the city, and he understood enough of it to realize that they were in panic.

"We should have left their animals! Now their God is following us! I told you so but ...no... you never listen to me," one of them yelled.

"Hold your tongue!" Shouted the older one. "What god worries with some animals?

A god only worries with what we give them but not what we take from others." "What do you know? I hear this God is another kind. It is a God that you cannot see but the Jewish people say he sees all things and is in all places at the same time!" the gruff and dirty robber said.

"What are you? Are you with us or are you a Jew too?" the leader of the group shouted and he pushed the two away. Before a real fight could break out, the wind blew again but this time the animals, all of them, broke loose and began bleating and running around. The wind grew stronger and stronger and one of the men grabbed his belongings and started running. One of the men followed his friend hurriedly but the rest continued trying to pull the animals along.

Everyone knows donkeys are stubborn and this one was no different. As the wind picked up even more and whistled through the trees, the donkey dug his four hooves into the dry dirt and gave a hollow bellow. It had a very spooky sound to it, even to the ears of Nebo! The thieves seemed to agree and without even grabbing their belongings, they ran off into the dark, cursing and yelling.

Ah-bee lunged forward and took the animals' ropes. They were subdued now and followed without any problems. Even the donkey cooperated. Each man took a rope from Ah-bee and the animals followed easily. They walked back to where they left the boys with the burning torch. The men used the remaining burning torch to light all their torches and soon all had lights again.

"Let's find our way back to the camp now," said Zerubbabel as he took the lead.

"It is going to take us a while," said Ah-bee to Nebo. "Are you ok?"

Nebo nodded. "I'm tired but I can still walk to the camp," he said.

They followed Zerubbabel and walked quietly until pale light broke the darkness.

Just when the first light of the sun began to peek over the horizon, they saw their camp in front of them. A loud celebration roared through the people when they spotted their men and the animals. The women and children ran out to greet their returning husbands and fathers.

They had been up the whole night praying and waiting, but now they were clapping and singing as the women brought flatbread and fig pasta to celebrate and have breakfast.

After the prayers of Jeshua, the leaders decided to resume their journey and move forward with extra speed. They quickly broke camp and started walking.

The following week the caravan continued moving at a rapid pace. The soldiers kept more guards on duty during the night hours and some of the leaders formed a watch group and took turns in the night. Soon Nebo was able to wriggle himself into this important position. This helped

his father who was very tired from a lack of sleep
at night, and his ongoing pastoral duties during
the day. Ah-bee was frequently sought out by
those who were feeling unsure about the future.
Many were concerned about how to find food and

how to survive in Jerusalem. He knew they were feeling uncertain, but Ah-bee kept telling them to trust Adonai, their God. "If God was bringing us back, He would surely provide," Ah-bee reassured them. "Remember the words of the Law:

when you and your children return to the LORD your God and obey Him with all your heart and with all your soul according to everything, I command you God will bless us."

CHAPTER 7:
On the Move Again

During the second month of the trip, they had to run off two more robbery attempts. Given that, as well as the seemingly unending journey, some people began to feel discouraged. At times, the leaders had to call in families to encourage them and, occasionally, even to rebuke them for talking against the word of God. God is surely good enough to take care of them.

All the people looked much leaner than when they left Babylon. The fun luxury foods like dates and pomegranates were long gone and the most they had to eat was flatbread with fish, sop and onions. But even that was going to come to an end soon.

Zerubbabel called a meeting and explained the terrain they would now be traveling. It would be hilly at first, and then mountains after that. This meant that for the first time during their travels there would not be the river to follow and thus, no fish, no fresh water to drink and no baths. "Water is precious and will soon be scarce," said Zerubbabel. "Fill all your jars with water. You will have to ration water." With worried faces, the people listened to him. Some shouted questions.

"We will stay in this place for one week so we can catch and dry enough fish for the days ahead. If any of you can hunt, please go do it. Then we must dry the meat. We might not be able to find food in the mountains and we will probably need to walk through the dry plains for some days too," warned Zerubbabel.

The intensity of the situation hit everyone suddenly. Ima quickly took measure of what she had left over for food. "I want you all to stay close to the tent and help me," she told her children. "Help me check the bags," she said to Nebo and the girls. Soon they had a good idea of what was left. "Ima, we have two whole bags with grains," said Nebo. "That is good," said Ima. "That is enough grain to make cakes and flatbread."

"And we have dried plums and dried apples," said Bilah, showing three basketfuls of dried fruits. "And a whole jar of onions and garlic." She continued to uncover the food and present it to her mother.

"Oh good, and we have here a small container honey left over and I have some spices," Ima pointed out.

"If we can get fish to dry and maybe hunt down a deer or so, that would be good," Nebo said. When Ah-bee arrived, they shared the food situation with him. He decided to slaughter two of the goats in order to start drying them. "We better make sure to have enough food," he said. "Some people in the caravan don't have much and we might need to share with them."

Everybody was on edge during that week and some discussions became very heated and had to be brought in front of the priests. Ah-bee was busier counseling the families than doing any other business. This meant Nebo was the lone fisherman for his family. Nebo was afraid when he went to the river the first day. It was certainly enjoyable to fish when he could do it with his father and use the fish for fun food. But to be responsible for feeding his whole family for the last part of the trip was something else. All the families had sent their boys to fish and Nebo went with his cousins up to the site allotted to his clan.

Before getting started, Nebo quietly went into the bushes and prayed to God. "Help me father to have enough food for my Ima and sisters. Ah-bee cannot help me but I need to bring enough food home." He wiped his eyes twice while he prayed. And then he went to work. Slowly and thoughtfully he lowered his line into the water, and it wasn't long before he caught his first fish. The success continued as he caught fish after fish, and before he knew it, he had twelve. Some of them were too big to fit in the basket his mother had given him that morning. "Yohoo," Nebo laughed as he continued working.

When he was finished, he praised the Lord as he walked back to the camp to deliver the fish to his mother so they could start cleaning and drying them. During the following days Nebo managed to catch enough fish to fill an entire clay jar with dried fish.

The men who went hunting shared pieces of meat with Ah-bee as part of their sacrifices and Ima was not worried anymore about food. She and the girls dug up some cassava roots, then cooked and dried them. During rough times, they could use it to make a type of a flatbread.

During these busy days, entire families were collecting food, then cooking, drying and storing it in such a way that the food would not go bad or be subjected to bugs. In the evenings when all the meat and fish hung to dry in the smoke, the families came together and were instructed in the laws of the Lord. Ah-bee went to great lengths to teach the clan. Some of the boys got lessons in Hebrews and everybody practiced the Hebrew language. Nebo decided to stop talking Aramaic altogether with his cousins so they could practice and speak Hebrew better.

When the caravan finally broke camp and was ready to move forward, it was with great sadness that the people looked back to the river. It had helped them to take care of their families for so long, and now that they were leaving the river, they were afraid of the hard times ahead.

CHAPTER 8

Water

The caravan moved forward, toward the Promised Land. One day at a time. One day became two days, and then three, and eventually it had been a week. Going through the hilly terrain was difficult. Even the animals suffered. After five days, Zerubbabel sent a message down the camp that they would take two days to rest. There were elder people who could not keep going. However, there was no water to be found in the hills and part of their group was eager to keep going. Some proposed to make two groups, one for the quick walkers and one for the slow walkers. "Do you dare to walk away from your elders?" an old man asked in a heated voice. Others agreed with him and the plan to leave the slow walkers behind was dropped.

The leaders decided that the group would not take extra rest days but that the elders would be carried on the makeshift carriers. So the group kept moving.

"Ima," said Nebo one day, worried. "I took the last water this morning from the black vat. What are we going to do?"

"I know son," said Ima with the same look of worry on her face. "I gave the last big jar today to the animals to drink. I think we have enough water for one more day and then we need to refill. Adonai will provide. We are surely not going to die of thirst," Ima said. They all laughed and that broke the tension.

"Ah-bee has been called to the front of the caravan for prayers this morning. Let's walk over there and pray with them," Nebo said and took Bilah by the hand. Ima left her tent and walked quickly with her children. Many people were already gathered in the prayer square. The word that was on every person's lips was "water." Water was indeed a hot issue.

Nebo, along with some of the other young people, prayed together. Ah-bee read from the

Word and the elders prayed. People were on their knees, crying out to God, asking Him to supply them.

Zerubbabel finally addressed the group and said, "I want some young strong men to form a group and go out into the mountains and try to find a waterfall or a river. Even a small river will do."

"But where will we find such a river?" called a young man. He clearly didn't want to go for such a dangerous task.

"I think you need to climb up to the highest spot on those mountains," said Zerubbabel and he pointed to a high mountain. "When you are high up there, look around. If you see any green in this brown country, there must be water and you need to find it."

Nebo laughed. He had not thought about that.

"I want to go," he called out.

"He can't go, he is only a boy. We need men to lead us in this adventure," said another.

"He is the son of the preacher and didn't he go and get our animals back when the robbers stole them?" another argued on Nebo's behalf. Others began to quarrel.

"Stop it!" said Zerubbabel frustrated. "If the boy wants to go, let him go. We need young, quick legs and an eager mind. And a pair of good eyes."

Soon more people joined and Zerubbabel appointed Akki as leader of the group. While they still had daylight, they quickly headed for the top of the mountain Zerubbabel had pointed out. In the meantime, Zerubbabel asked all the people to check their water supply and to share with family members who didn't have enough for that day.

They did as they were told and all the people and animals in the camp got enough water before heading back to their tents to pray and hope. It would be at least half a day before the young men would come back, so Ah-bee sat at the entrance of his tent with his head bowed, his prayer shawl over his head, and prayed.

It hadn't been long when, to their surprise, they heard loud noises and shouts coming from the directions of the mountains. The scouting group was already coming back. "Ah-bee!" yelled Nebo as he ran to his father. "We didn't need to go all the way up. We could clearly see a very green spot not far from here. Zerubbabel has sent orders to break camp and walk there before dark."

Ah-bee and Ima hugged Nebo, then with quick hands, they packed the animals and broke camp. Everyone was eager to find fresh water.

They walked for hours but just before it turned dark, they came upon the river. It was actually more of a spring coming forth from a dark rock formation. Zerubbabel tasted the water first and declared it drinkable. "Yehhhhheeeeee,

Praise God, Our God is good, his promises are for always," the people were saying as they found a place at the bank of the river to fill their vats. Water had never tasted so good. That same night the young people took the chance to get into the water to wash themselves, and most of the camp followed suit the next morning. The fresh water was so refreshing – both to the body and to the soul.

Nebo refilled all the vats for Ima and he let the animals get fresh water too.

They spent the whole next day camping next to the river and nobody felt like leaving the river, but they knew they had to. The hardest part of the crossing would start now. They needed to cross the plains.

After two days, they left the rock formations behind and were once again in flat country. However, this time, with no river.

Zerubbabel called a meeting again and explained "The temperatures in these plains can rise extremely during the day and the nights can be very chilly. I suggest we change our walking schedule. Let's get up very early and start walking at

four o'clock in the morning and then walk until it is too hot to walk. Then we will camp and try to sleep. When it cools back off, we'll continue walking in the evening until late. This way, we will escape the heat a little."

That was exactly what the people did.

Nebo had never walked in hot plains before and he was surprised at the flatness and sandiness of the land. Within one hour, the sand had penetrated everything. "Ah-bee, I have sand between my teeth and in my ears," Nebo said annoyed. Ah-bee was using his prayer shawl to keep that sand from getting into his eyes and nose. The wind didn't help much. It was a hot and uncomfortable wind. It didn't bring cooling but swept the sand up into all the crevices and hollows of all the people and their possessions. The animals were quite annoyed too as they kept moving their ears and tail in a futile attempt to keep the sand away.

The voyage in the plains was indeed slower and the water supply went quickly, but on the fifth day of the trip into the plains, they came upon the country of another clan of people. Their city was built behind a rock formation, and it was cooler. A river brought refreshment for them. The Jews asked and received permission to refill their water vats. Zerubbabel wanted to call a three-day rest and everybody enjoyed that idea but after prayer, Jeshua, the high priest, decided against it. They would move on the next day.

It turned out to be one day too late though. Something terrible happened that night. Maybe it was due to fatigue, or maybe it was the peacefulness of the country, but the men who were meant to protect their goods were not as alert that night. Nobody had heard or seen anything but to everybody's disbelief, the robbers managed to steal many containers of dried food and even some goats. Ima was crying. All her fish were gone.

Ah-bee looked down and didn't say much. He pulled his prayer shawl over his head.

"I'm not sure we will have enough food left over for the trip," said Ima, and Nebo felt bad.

"We can always kill a cow Ima," he said, trying to cheer her up.

"We need them for Jerusalem, my son. They will give us cheese, and the milk we need for drinking. Remember that Jerusalem is empty no roads, no stores, nowhere to buy or trade anything. All we will have is here with us."

"And we need animals to sacrifice son. That is the only way we have to pay our sinful debts with the Lord," Ah-bee said.

Nebo looked down. He knew all of this; there was just nothing he could say or do.

"Do we still have vegetables?" Bilah asked, and Ima looked into the bags. She found a bundle of carrots, a bag of onions and some garlic. There were some dried apricots left, and figs too, but not much more. There was also enough flour for some flatbread. Nebo continued helping Ima look through the many bags and storage boxes. Suddenly he jumped up, with a big bag in his hand, "I found nuts!" he said. "Pistachio nuts!" and everybody laughed.

Then with a smirk on his face, Ah-bee said, "As the head of this house, I need to taste these nuts first to make sure they are good before I can give some to my family," and he stretched out his hands. "Yeah right," said Nebo but he still gave his father a fist full. Then Ima and his sisters wanted some too and on this happy note, the family went to bed.

CHAPTER 9

Pushing Forward

The next day they washed all their clothes and took a bath in the river. Then they walked upstream were they took fresh water for the road. With this, they were ready to continue the trip.

Zerubbabel spoke with the leaders and explained the last part of the trip. It would be a very difficult part of the journey, but after crossing the last part of the plains, they would be in the Promised Land!

With Zerubbabel in the lead, the caravan left the green and lush oasis and started their long trek back home.

Despite the heat, dust and lack of food, they kept pushing forward. There was just not much anybody could do about the elements, so they kept putting one foot in front of the other and trudged on. They tried to shield their faces from the sun and dust as much as possible, and in the night, they stayed warm by sleeping together and taking turns keeping guard to protect their possessions.

One morning Nebo was watching Ah-bee as he recorded the new day. "Why do you write down all the days Ah-bee?" he asked.

"We need to know when we left and when we arrived there, son," Ah-bee said. "And I need to know when it's the Sabbath. We need to observe the Sabbath carefully. That is why I make sure that we keep track of the days." Nebo understood the importance of this task and admired his father for his diligence and responsibility.

Their journey continued, and the days became weeks and the weeks became months. But finally, on the first day of the seventh month, just when they came around a significant rock formation, a rumble of excitement worked its way through the caravan. "Israel!" Children and elders alike started running and jumping around.

Nebo ran to his father. "Ah-bee may I go to the front of the caravan to see it?"

Laughing, Ah-bee gave permission. He wanted to go to the front too, but he could not as he noticed many of the family heads were moving in his direction to seek more information.

Suddenly the caravan stopped and a runner approached Ah-bee, asking him to come to a meeting with the elders at the front of the caravan. Ah-bee went with Nebo. More people were moving to the front of the caravan. This was sure to be an important meeting.

Zerubbabel was already there praying with some of the men. The sun was high and for the first time Nebo could see the beginning of Israel civilization in the distance.

"We are soon coming up to the Jordan River," said Zerubbabel at that moment. "We will follow it down until we reach Jericho and then we will cross. If we cross too early, we will be in the Samaritan territory and we don't want that. They have never kept a clean religion and I don't want to make us all impure just before entering Jerusalem." Everybody agreed with him.

So it was decided that they would walk a few more hours that day and try to reach the Jordan River by nightfall. Once there, they would get water to wash and purify themselves before entering the Holy Land.

Soon the caravan was in step again. The singers sang and the group moved forward at top speed. Nobody complained or quarreled that day and they maintained focus. It was already after dark when they arrived at the riverbank and with torches blazing to give light, they made their camp.

CHAPTER 10:

Crossing into the Promised Land

They woke up early the next morning and walked the bank, looking around. The river was swollen and roaring. Nebo looked at it with big eyes. This river looked nothing like the one they had back home. He grasped his father's hand and looked up with wide eyes, "There's no way we can get to the other side, Ah-bee, and how about Saba and the animals? They cannot swim."

Ah-bee nodded. "Sure looks impossible," he said while twisting his beard. "But we, the Jews, have a great history with water parting for the people to cross. So it's important that we trust the Lord and pray about it."

"Do you mean when the Red Sea parted, Ah-bee?" asked Nebo and Ah-bee nodded. "But Moses was there when that happened, and we don't have Moses with us now."

"No, we don't have Moses, but still the same God," said Ah-bee with conviction. "God is our hero, he will make a way. We just need to trust. And... maybe you should stop looking at the river," he teased when he saw that Nebo was looking doubtfully at the high river.

Later that morning, Jeshua proclaimed a day of fasting and prayers and everybody complied. They washed all they had and washed themselves ceremonially. In the evening, they confessed their sins to the priest and offered some animals as sacrifice. All was well.

The next day the river was even higher than the day before and many people came to Ah-bee asking what should be done now. Some people openly complained. Jeshua declared another day of fasting and sacrifices and the complainers had to come before the leaders.

Jeshua spoke with the whole group. "Brothers and sisters. Please do not complain. Use your time wisely. Pray to God and ask him to calm the river so we can cross. I want us all to offer sacrifices and to confess our complaining and to ask God for a way to cross. We need to trust that God will do this for us." That night the people were peaceful. The complaining stopped, and men were sitting silently with prayer shawls over their heads.

Ah-bee walked among the people and encouraged all. Some boys went to fish and for the first time in many days, they could smell fish frying over hot coals. All was well in the camp.

These two types of fishes lives in the Jordan River.
These are the fishes they were eating.

Nebo woke up early the next morning and realized a familiar noise he'd heard for the last couple of days was gone. He didn't know what the missing sound was, so he left the tent in search of Ah-bee. He found Ah-bee standing outside with his hands stretched in the air. "Morning Ah-bee. What is going on?" he asked.

"Listen," said Ah-bee, "do you hear that?" "I don't hear anything," said Nebo.

"Exactly!" said Ah-bee. "I don't hear the river. Let's go look."

Quickly they moved between the many tents and crossed through the trees.

Usually the noise of the river would have been loud by now but an eerie silence hung in the air.

Nebo reached the riverbank first and couldn't believe his eyes. The roaring river from the day before had shrunk into a trickle of water. Even the elderly would be able to just wade over!

"Oh Ah-bee!" shouted Nebo. "God did it for us! We can cross now. God is good. He listened to our prayers."

Ah-bee was wiping his eyes and praising God at the same time. They immediately went to wake up the rest of the camp and preparations were made for the morning prayers of thanks and for a quick breakfast. Then it was time to start with the crossing. It was not easy to get so many people and animals across the river, and it took many hours and lots of helping hands. Nebo joined the men and strong boys as they stood in two lines, forming a path down the middle. As the people walked between the two human walls, every man within the human wall stuck out his hands to assist those who were walking by. In order to keep their goods dry, they passed bags and vessels from hand-to-hand to get them to the other side. When the last was safe at the side of the Holy Land, the men and boys followed. It took the group the entire day to cross the river with all their goods and animals, just in time to pitch the tents and go to evening's prayer. Jeshua proclaimed a fast of thanksgiving for the next day and a long reading of the scrolls. It was a joyous evening. Although it was already dark, nobody wanted to go to their tents so they stayed up, clapping and singing worship until late.

The next day, they worshipped the Lord all day, read the scripture and sacrificed again.

It was already quite late when Ah-bee came to walk with Nebo. It was almost dark but together they climbed a rock and stood there, looking afar. Ah-bee had a bag with him.

"Tomorrow we will go into our new country, son," Ah-bee said. "It is now too dark to see anything but I promise you that this is a glorious country. Our God gave it to us and we will prosper here. Do you remember the words of the law that I made you memorize?"

"Yes Ah-bee," said Nebo and stood erect to recite the words.

*"When you and your children return
to the Lord your God and obey him
with all your heart and with all
your soul according to everything I
command you today, ³ then the Lord
your God will restore your fortunes
and have compassion on you and
gather you again from all the nations
where he scattered you."*

Ah-bee slapped him on the shoulder.

"That is the way to go, son. Hide all God's words in your heart and live them. Do you also remember what God will do when you obey him?"

Expectantly he looked Nebo in the eyes. Nebo realized that this was very important to Ah-bee. It was like a test of all Ah-bee had taught him on the way to the new land. He smiled slowly, stood erect and said, "The LORD your God will circumcise your hearts and the hearts of your descendants, so that you may love Him with all your heart and with all your soul, and live."

A visibly emotional Ah-bee hugged Nebo.

"That's it, son! You are ready for the new country. You are ready to serve God in this new land God gave us, Jerusalem, our Promised Land."

Ah-bee opened his bag and produced their sleeping mats. "We will sleep here tonight," he said. "That way we can see Jerusalem from here in the morning." They rolled out their sleeping mats and slept under the clear sky of their new land. Father and son. Ready for a new adventure.

The next morning they got up very early while it was still dark. They prayed together as they waited for the sun to come up over the horizon and light up the pale sky. When the sun finally rose, Ah-bee pointed to the high mountains, standing upright and powerful, off in the distance. "Son, look up!" Ah-bee shouted, overwhelmed with emotion. "There is Jerusalem, our city. We made it, we are home!"

Nebo looked at Jerusalem, high in the mountains and a warm feeling filled his heart. Beaming with a sense of pride and excitement, he said to his father, "We did it Ah-bee; we are in the Promised Land."